Original title: Plaisirs de Chats
Design and graphic realization:
Jean-Marc Côté
Published by La Courte Échelle
Montréal, Québec

A FRIEND LIKE YOU

Roger Paré

English text by David Homel

Annick Press
Toronto, Canada

One-two-three,
Come and dance
With me.

A flower here,
A flower there.
A yellow flower
For your hair.

Let me sing
A little song,
A tune to last
The whole night long.

Rocking with you,
talking with you,
A warm summer's day
with you.

In the woods
The sun shines through,
As I walk
Along with you.

Purple, yellow,
Red and blue,
You draw me
And I'll draw you.

Apple cheeks,
Apple pie,
You're the apple
Of my eye.

Bedtime, sleepy time,
I love story time.

Birds and rabbits
Say hello
As we glide
Across the snow.

I'm glad I have a friend
Like you,
To cuddle up
The whole night through.

Annick Press gratefully acknowledges the support of The Canada Council.

Canadian Cataloguing in Publication Data

Paré, Roger
    [Plaisirs de chats. English]
    A friend like you

Translation of: Plaisirs de chats.
ISBN 0-920303-04-8 (bound) — 0-920303-05-6 (pbk.)

I. Title. II. Title: Plaisirs de chats. English.

PS8581.A697P513 1984   jC843'.54   C84-098924-5
PZ7.P375Fr 1984

Distributed in Canada and the USA by:
Firefly Books Ltd.
3520 Pharmacy Ave., Unit 1c
Scarborough, Ontario
M1W 2T8

Printed and bound in Canada by
D.W. Friesen & Sons Ltd.